A. L Slawson

Behind the scenes; or, An expose of Oneida community. :

Embracing their social and sexual relations, spiritual controls,

origin, and a brief sketch of its founder ..

A. L Slawson

Behind the scenes; or, An expose of Oneida community. : Embracing their social and sexual relations, spiritual controls, origin, and a brief sketch of its founder ..

ISBN/EAN: 9783741166266

Manufactured in Europe, USA, Canada, Australia, Japa

Cover: Foto ©Andreas Hilbeck / pixelio.de

Manufactured and distributed by brebook publishing software
(www.brebook.com)

A. L Slawson

Behind the scenes; or, An expose of Oneida community. : Embracing their social and sexual relations, spiritual controls, origin, and a brief sketch of its founder ..

BEHIND THE SCENES;

OR,

An Exposé

OF

ONEIDA COMMUNIT

EMBRACING

Y

Their Social and Sexual Relations, Spiritual **Controls**, Origin,

AND

A BRIEF SKETCH OF ITS FOUNDEI

"IN HOLY PHRASE TRANSACTED VILLANIES
THAT COMMON SINNERS DURST NOT MEDDLE WITH."

ONEIDA, N. Y.:
A. L. SLAWSON, PUBLISHER.
MDCCCLXXV.

PREFACE.

In the following pages will be found matters not merely of local interest, but of vital import to the nation. Here in the very heart of advanced civilization, under the patronage of some of our best citizens, an institution is spreading which is as shameless as the "mother of harlots and abominations," and as corrupt as the lowest bawd-house in the land. With these remarks I submit my unpretending work to the consideration of the reader, with an earnest desire that it may prove of some benefit in a work of reform which must soon be commenced.

THE AUTHOR.

ONEIDA, N. Y., March, 1875.

ONEIDA COMMUNITY.

CHAPTER I.

BRIEF DESCRIPTION OF BUILDINGS—LANDS—NUM-
BER OF MEMBERS—FINANCIAL AFFAIRS—WIL-
LOW PLACE COMMUNITY—DRESS OF THE MEM-
BERS.

THE lands belonging to Oneida Community lie
principally in the town of Lenox, Madison County,
New York, about four miles south of the thriving
village of Oneida, a small part only—that
known as "Willow Community," lying in the
County of Oneida. The estate, which consists of 600
acres, is what was once an Indian reservation, and
is nearly one mile in extent from north to south.
Through this vast tract the New York and Oswego
Midland Railroad runs nearly the whole length, the
station near the mansion being known as that of
Oneida Community. When the Community started
here, some twenty-seven years ago, its capital was

one hundred thousand dollars, invested in lands, buildings, &c. For a few years it was not success-ful, financially, and the capital of the concern de-creased from that sum to forty thousand dollars. Then, owing to better management, things took an upward turn, until the money now invested in lands and buildings amounts to nearly half a million dol-lars and the property is steadily increasing.

From a quartet, consisting of J. H. Noyes and wife and one Cragin and wife, mentioned in another part of this work, has sprung a community to-day numbering 253 members, and which is spreading with a rapidity well calculated to excite grave ap-prehensions in the minds of all who have the wel-fare of mankind at heart, and which appeals to every lover of morality for aid in the suppression of its contaminating influences.

The buildings consist of the mansion, Tontine, trap shop, silk factory and Willow Place residence. The "mansion" is a brick building, trimmed with stone, has a large "upright" and two wings sur-mounted with towers, and a Mansard, or French roof. This is devoted to offices ; the "family" hall, where the family meet for social exercises and "criticism ;" the upper sitting-room ; the library, containing about four hundred volumes ; the Mu-seum, a slimly supplied affair, and the ordinary rooms of a family. The large brick building, called the "Tontine," is located a few yards west of the mansion, with which it is connected by an underground passage. The basement of the "Tontine" is used for the various domestic duties of the Community—cooking, washing, &c. The family hall is located in the mansion, and is arranged with seats, stage, &c., like an ordinary public hall, and here all the members meet for social enjoyment or the settlement of any individual grievance which may grow out of the "complex" system from time to time.

To show the manner in which business is conducted, we copy the following from the *Circular* of January 25, 1875, although anything pertaining to their financial or business interests may properly be considered as digressing from the subject of this book :

"As our business affairs are now organized, we have a busy time at the beginning of each year. During the last week of December every department is hard at work getting out its annual inventory ; these must all be completed, verified, and handed into the General Office on or before the evening of December 31, as the books are then closed for the year. The trial-balances to test the accuracy of the books follow as at the beginning of every month. As soon as the books are thus proved the general balance-sheet is made out, which shows us exactly what we have earned during the past year. A full statement of all our expenses and income is read in General Assembly. Then comes the important question as to how we shall invest or expend the balance of earnings.

"General notice is given that any member who has in mind any project, public or private, requiring money, should now make a written application for such sum as he or she may desire to expend. The managers of the various businesses are also expected to apply for such increased capital as may be needed to meet an increasing trade. Numerous and various are the projects for which money is asked. The applications, being filed, make a respectable volume. To show the range of projects which the Financial Board are called on to consider and furnish with funds, we give a list of the matters for which money was asked by one and another this year:

" Agricultural Improvements ; Study of Botany ; Bedding ; Bridge ; Improving Cellar Windows ; Bidet ; Photographic Camera and Burnishing Machine ; Boat ; Stage Curtain ; Children's Play-House ; Carpentry Improvements ; Cresting on Roof ; Scientific Experiments ; Carpets, Wall Paper, etc. ; Case of Drawers ; New Dental Chair ; Door ; Deer Park ; Earth Closets ; Extinguishing Fires ; Garden Arbor ; Tools ; New Furniture ; To light our buildings by Gas ; Greenhouse ; Hardware ; Hospital ; House for Paper Rags; Ice House at Villa; "Keep"; Landscape Improvements ; Library ; Medical Books; Museum ; Magic Lantern ; Mineralogy and Geology ; New Office ; Painting ; Personal Expenses ; Heating Apparatus ; Repairs on Buildings ; Refrigerator ; Rotary Oven ; Water Filters ; Spectroscope ; Sewing

Machine; Chimney; Sink; Silver-Plated Knives; School-Room Improvements; Toys; Dental Tools; Taxidermy; Turkish Bath; Harness; Coal Yard; Law Books; Wash-Room; Steam Boiler; Steam Trap; Philosophical Department; Silk Capital; Bath-Room Improvements; Umbrella Cupboard; New Ventilator; Watches; Water Supply; Wax Flowers; Wardrobes; Writing Machine; New Windows; Repairs to Water Powers and Steam Powers, etc.

"To treat all such applications in a way to subserve the best interests of the Community, and yet to satisfy the applicants, requires long and studious deliberations through many sittings of the Financial Board. The sum total asked for is sometimes in excess of the amount ready for disposal. This necessitates a careful pruning of the projects by the Board. When they have adjusted the appropriations to the best of their ability the list is read in one of our meetings, and either approved or corrected by the family vote. This plan of expending our earnings works quite smoothly, and is especially valuable as a method of correcting the tendency to expend one's income in anticipation of receiving it."

The men of the Community are permitted to dress as they choose, and in this matter do not differ materially from ordinary people, their tastes being nearly as diversified. The women, however, have adopted a sort of "bloomer" costume, the dress reaching to the knees, terminating with a close-fit-

ting straight *pantalette*, which reaches to the top of
the shoes. They are quite plainly attired, and from
the dejected and care-worn appearance of most o
them, it is undoubtedly a God-send that, whatever
of personal attraction they may possess, they do not
heighten it with the dress of modern female society.
Some idea of their appearance can be gained from
the illustration given of the "Quadrangle," when
there is a promiscuous assemblage of both visitors
and members of the Community.

WILLOW PLACE COMMUNITY, an offshoot of the
parent tree of corruption, is located one and a quarter miles north of the Community proper. It has
nineteen members, each one of whom has been selected by the faithful to perform the office of beget-
ting offspring in accordance with the principles of
"male continence," of which subject we shall have
occasion to speak more fully hereafter. The trap-
shop and silk factory are located at this place, under
the supervision of two leading "Brothers." The
labor in these manufactories is carried on by people
from the adjacent village of Oneida, who are con-
veyed to and from their work in three large omni-
buses, built with especial reference to the business.
Although this branch is called "Willow Place," it
is nothing more nor less than the detachment of a
few whose natures are not in accord with the multi-
tudes on the "social system" of Bible communism
or complex marriage, as adopted by the mass of the
members, or, in other words, who are too selfish to

mingle with the common horde in their lasciviousness. More plainly still, they are a privileged few who have banded together for the better gratification of their sexual desires, while their duties are ostensibly to superintend the manufacturing interests of the Community.

CHAPTER II.

Its Origin—Brief Biographical Sketch of its
Founder—The Rout at Putney—Noyes In-
dicted for Incest and Fornication—He is
Held to Bail and Runs Away—The Battle-
Axe Letter.

Community life began at Putney, Vt., in the year
1846, but the people of that place, foreseeing the
evil consequences of the doctrines of communistic
ideas, at once routed its disciples and drove them to
seek quarters in this State, where, in the year 1848,
Oneida Community was founded.   The germ of this
unholy "ism" was planted in rich soil, as the financial condition of the concern most fully attests, and
that it had for its head and front a man of more than
ordinary ability and culture, a brief sketch of J. H.
Noyes' life will amply testify.   John Humphrey
Noyes was born at West Brattleboro, Vt., Sept. 3,
1811.   He was the eldest son of John and Polly
Noyes.   His father was a man of respectable talents,
and in early life proposed to enter the Christian
ministry.   He subsequently abandoned the idea,
however, and devoted himself to mercantile pur-
suits, in which, for many years, he was extensively
engaged.   Being successful in business, he accumu-
lated considerable property and subsequently ac-

quired some political distinction, being a representative in Congress in 1816 from the Southern Congressional District of Vermont. He became a resident of Putney about the year 1823, where he lived up to the time of his death, which occurred in 1841. At his decease the lawful heirs to his estate, consisting of three sons and three daughters, inherited each a handsome patrimony. And Rev. Hubbard Eastman, his biographer, adds, "Thus it appears that the founder of the sect of Perfectionists had a respectable and even somewhat honorable parentage." J. H. Noyes graduated at Dartmouth College in 1830, being then nineteen years of age. Soon after leaving college he commenced the study of the law. After having studied law about one year, or, in 1831, his attention was directed to religious subjects, and he soon after made a profession of religion at a protracted meeting held in Putney, and became a member of the Congregational Church in that town. After uniting with the Church he determined on entering the ministry, and commenced his studies preparatory to engaging in that work. In about four weeks from the time of his professed conversion he entered the Theological Seminary, at Andover, Mass., where he remained one year, and then went to New Haven, Ct., and entered the Theological Seminary, connected with Yale College, in the Fall of 1832. In August, 1833, he was licensed to preach by the New Haven Association. After receiving license he labored for six weeks as pastor of a small church in

North Salem, N. Y. In February, 1834, he came out a Perfectionist. Soon after this event he was ex-communicated from the Congregational Church in Putney, of which he had been a member, for heresy and breach of covenant. "Noyes," says the Rev. Mr. Hubbard, "having lost most of his influence at New Haven, left that place and spent considerable time in traveling in different parts of the country." During this time he made a few converts to his faith, but in 1838 he returned to Putney and resumed the publication of a paper called *The Witness*, which had been suspended about a year previous, in con-sequence of the odium brought down upon it by the publication of the "Battle-Axe Letter," which will be given further on.

Almost from the commencement of Noyes' pecu-liar doctrine there had been occasional demonstra-tions made by the populace of Putney and vicinity against some of the number who adhered to them, which at first led Noyes to deny that the frequent violations of moral and statute law were the fruits thereof, and to attribute them to spurious doctrines which some had introduced. He did not evidently consider it safe then to openly proclaim what he since has in regard to his principles of Perfectionism.

As he grew more bold in expressing and enforcing his views, the citizens of Putney went to work in earnest, and in 1847, October 25th, he was arrested, charged with *adultery* and *fornication*, and a true bill was found against him by the grand jury on the charges preferred. In September, 1848, the case was called in the Windham County Court, but Noyes did not appear, having fled the country and forfeited his bail, giving as an excuse for this course that he "could do better than engage in a small quarrel with an excited village;" and no one will be apt to dispute him. The near prospect of being encompassed by granite walls and looking through iron grates, was a very good stage of the proceedings at which to become "peaceable and non-resistant," even though at the time of his arrest he is said to have "roared like a lion at the end of his chain."

Shortly after the event narrated, Noyes issued a 96-page pamphlet, in which he gave a "Confession of Religious Experience," and also drew up a long article entitled "Institutions and Organization of the Kingdom of Heaven," which he sent to the believers at Putney, with instructions to show it to sincere inquirers, and which they claimed to be of divine inspiration.

Some of the most prominent members still remaining at Putney after Noyes had absconded, and the publication of their *Spiritual Magazine* still being continued, and to which Noyes in his exile contributed his pernicious articles, in December, 1847, a public indignation meeting was held in that village to take into consideration the outrageous proceedings of the so-called Perfectionists. At this meeting a set of preambles and resolutions were adopted which declared that all prudent and lawful measures should be resorted to by the people to vindicate the rights of the injured, bring the guilty to justice, and remove the gangrene which had fastened upon the morals of that community. These expressions of the citizens of Putney had the effect of dampening the ardor of the few remaining followers of Noyes, and the removal of the *Spiritual Magazine* to what was then known as Oneida Reserve—now Oneida Community—whither he had fled, and, with the sainted Cragin, established his temple.

With this rough outline of the doings of the Perfectionists at Putney, we are brought down to the Community as it exists at the present day. The publication of the *Spiritual Magazine* was discontinued, and *The Oneida Circular* took its place, which publication is still continued. Like its predecessor, the pernicious doctrines of Perfectionism are still advocated as boldly and indecently as ever. As we shall show by excerpts from its pages, its publication would not be tolerated in the tainted atmosphere of a city, even for a single month.

As the reader will naturally desire to know something of the peculiar *religious* doctrines of the Communists, the famous " Battle-Axe Letter "—so called from being published in a paper called *The Battle-Axe*—will serve in place of any comments of our own, and much better than anything we have been able to find in the published works of the sect. In the following extract will be found the substance of the letter, or that portion of it upon which rests the most debasing and licentious institution under the sun-light of Heaven. He says :

"I will write all that is in my heart on one delicate subject, and you may judge for yourself whether it is expedient to show this letter to others. When the will of God is done on Earth as it is in Heaven, *there will be no marriage.* The marriage supper of the Lamb is a feast at which *every dish is free to every guest.* Exclusiveness, jealousy, quarreling, have no place there, for the same reason as that which forbids the guests at a thanksgiving dinner to claim each his separate dish, and quarrel with the rest for his rights. *In a holy community there is no more reason why sexual intercourse should be restrained by law, than why eating and drinking should be,* and *there is as little occasion for shame in the one case as in the other.* God has placed a wall of partition between the male and the female during the apostasy, for good reasons, which will be broken down in the resurrection, for equally good reasons. But woe to him who abolishes the law of the apostasy before he stands in the holiness of the resurrection. The guests of the marriage supper may have each his favorite dish, each a dish of his own procuring, and that without the jealousy of exclusiveness. *I call a certain woman my wife—she is yours, she is Christ's, and in him she is the bride of* ALL SAINTS. She is dear in the hand of a stranger, and according to my promise to her I rejoice. My claim upon her cuts directly across the marriage covenant of this world, and God knows the end."

This letter was written in Ithaca, N. Y., and addressed to David Harrison of Meriden, Ct. After passing round among a few Perfectionists, it fell into the hands of Theophilus R. Gates of Philadelphia, who published it in the *Battle-Axe* of that city, without the knowledge of Noyes, who was not a little chagrined at its sudden appearance. But in the *Witness* of Sept. 2, 1837, published at Ithaca, N.Y., before Noyes had removed to Putney, he speaks of its publication as follows:

"As I am not responsible for the consequences of its *publication*, I might easily escape in a measure the fury of the storm which must follow it, but I choose to 'bide its brunt,' and therefore say that *I know the doctrine of that letter is* GOD'S *truth, and that whosoever contends with it, 'rushes upon the thick bosses* of HIS *buckler.'*

"As to the expediency of its publication *at the present time*, I say nothing. God understands his own business, and I leave it with Him and T. R. Gates to settle that matter. One thing I know, viz.: that before the will of God is done on earth, as it is in Heaven, that doctrine will be preached upon the house-tops."

In an article which appeared in the *Spiritual Magazine*, August 5, 1848, Noyes reviews the dispersion of his band at Putney the previous Fall, and speaks of his new location at Oneida as follows:

"We find ourselves now, after a short interval of comfortable confusion, by the invitation and cordial co-operation of Mr. Jonathan Burt and others of this vicinity, in a position much better than Putney ever gave us. * * * * Our dispersion last Fall, and the revolution among believers generally, resulting from the new position of our cause, have opened and warmed many hearts, as the varied correspondence presented in this paper shows."

Thus it will be seen that Noyes and his associates considered themselves well settled in this new location, which was termed the "Heavenly Association of Central New York," and measures were at once taken to raise the necessary means for its maintenance. All the leading spirits of the Putney Association were transferred to this new paradise, and it has since flourished like most seed of the devil's planting.

The peculiar *religion* of the Community is thus set forth in the *Circular :*

" The O. C. and Branches are not ' Free Lovers,' in the popular sense of the term. They call their social system BIBLE COMMUNISM or COMPLEX MARRIAGE, and hold to freedom of love only within their own families, subject to Free Criticism and the principles of Male Continence. In respect to permanency, responsibility, and every essential point of difference between marriage and licentiousness, the Oneida Communists stand with marriage. Free Love with them does *not* mean freedom to love to-day and leave to-morrow; nor freedom to take a woman's person and keep their property to themselves; nor freedom to freight a woman with offspring and send

her down stream without care or help; nor freedom
to beget children and leave them to the street and
the poor-house. Their Communities are *families*,
as distinctly bounded and separated from promiscuous society as ordinary households. The tie that
binds them together is as permanent and sacred, to
say the least, as that of marriage, for it is their religion. They receive no new members (except by
deception or mistake), who do not give heart and
hand to the family interest for life and forever.
Community of property extends just as far as freedom of love. Every man's care and every dollar of
the common property are pledged for the maintenance and protection of the women and children of
the Community."

;CHAPTER III.

SPIRITUAL "CONTROLS"—SELECTION BY "SIGNALS"
—THE FIRST STEP—THE KINGDOM OF HEAVEN
ESTABLISHED ON EARTH BY THE ADULTEROUS
INTERCOURSE OF NOYES AND THE CRAGINS—
"FOUR HANDS ROUND."

That the principle of "male continence" may be
thoroughly understood by the reader, the following
extracts have been taken from the same source.
We are painfully aware that such sensual articles
will not prove very entertaining to any but the most
sensualized minds, but it must be borne in mind
that mere *assertions* of the licentiousness of these
people will be no *proof* of their guilt. For this
reason, and without any desire to cater to a morbid
appetite for venal and obscene literature, it has
been thought prudent to give their own words, as
published in the exponent of their principles—the
Oneida Circular. Their social relations are grounded
upon the (to them) great principle of "male continence," of which Noyes claims to be the discoverer,
subject to "controls," which are defined by a writer
in the paper alluded to, in its issue of November 2,
1874, copied, it will be seen, from several editions.

The sale of the *Circular* which contained the "experience" given further on, was so great that the edition was exhausted without supplying the demand, and it was subsequently reprinted. Does any intelligent reader suppose for a moment that people purchased the paper from any *religious* or moral incentive, or that the object of its publishers in printing such filth, sprung from anything but the most debasing sensuality? It is certainly curious, to say the least, that their publications, which are daily becoming more bestial, are not frowned down by decent society, and that they have not long since been called to account by both the State and United States governments for their open violation of law, in circulating them broadcast over the country.

What words can be employed to depict the awfulness of an obscenity which throws around itself the garb of religion; which mingles with the coarsest vulgarity the name of the Most Omnipotent? Why do they crouch behind the name of religion in their nefarious practices? The answer is very plain—any other course would subject them to summary extermination; but the dodge of religion serves them as a bulwark, from behind which they can launch out their demoralizing doctrines with comparative safety; for, if they are attacked, the piteous cry of "persecution" can be raised, and they are at once transformed into religious martyrs. But, to return to the subject, the "controls" which guide the members of the Community, more espe-

cially those of the higher type of spirituality, are
thus lucidly explained :

[*From the Circular, Sept.* 14.]

* * * * * "John H. Noyes is a man who
claims to have lived and labored for the past forty
years under the guidance of an intelligent, invisible
control, which has inspired him with new thoughts,
and new truths, and given him the courage to proclaim them to the world. Do any doubt this?
Study his career. He has undoubtedly published
more new and important truths than any other
living man. On the old Bible doctrines, under the
guidance of his control, he has built up a new platform for Christian life, adapted to the times we live
in. His discovery about Christ's Second Coming,
the doctrines of Salvation from Sin, Mutual Criticism, Male Continence, Complex Marriage, Ascend-
ing Fellowship, Stirpiculture, etc., all relate to the
problems of human life in which everybody is most
interested. They also are in direct opposition to the
traditions and teachings of all divines and commen-
tators, and especially to all public opinion and
fashion. Nevertheless they thrive and are spreading. I have selected Mr. Noyes as an example because he acknowledges his control more explicitly
than any other man I know, always crediting his
discoveries, as did Paul, to Jesus Christ. He admits
that he is a better, stronger, more original and inde-

pendent man under his control than he could eve
have become without it." *   *   *   *   *   *

[*From the Circular, Sept.* 21.]

*   *   * " I referred last week to Mr. Noyes as an
instance of a man who has acted with perfect confidence under a particular spiritual control for many
years, submitting to that control the decision of all
his important affairs. He has been so uniformly
successful that it will be well worth while to understand his method of communicating with the spirit
which directs him. Here is his explanation of his
own experience:

"The exact methods by which spirits operate on
mortals in the various phases of what is called inspiration, is a very interesting subject of inquiry.
Judging by my own experience, I should define one
of the most important methods of spirit-leading as
selection by signals. This may seem rather a blind
formula, but I will make it clear by a very simple
illustration. The ordinary method of receiving
communications in Spiritualist circles has been by
calling the alphabet and getting raps at the letters
required. Here the thing done on one side is the
presentation of twenty-six symbols to be selected
from, and on the other an indication of the one
symbol selected by a sound. This is *selection by
signals* in the crudest form. Now, compare with
this the following more complicated process: In

some emergency of life I am at a loss what to do ;
I close my eyes and turn to Heaven for guidance ;
then I begin revolving in my mind all the possible
methods of action that might be taken ; when I
come to a certain mental proposal I feel a thrill of
assent and see a flash of fitness that makes me
sure instantaneously that I have found the course
that Heaven has chosen for me. What is this but
selection by signals? My revolving the various
possible courses is the equivalent of calling the
alphabet, and the thrill of assent is the equivalent
of the rap. Now I have to confess that this process has been the habit of my life for forty years.
I have found my way in this manner through all
vicissitudes. In this way I have chosen my beliefs. This is what I call "waiting on the Lord."
This is what I principally mean when I claim inspiration and talk about being " led by the Spirit."
And the more I reflect, the more I am inclined to
believe that all the processes of inspiration, in the
Bible and out of it, are resolvable at last into this
simple operation—*selection by signals.* The things
done on one side and the other may vary infinitely.
Instead of the slow calling of the alphabet there
may be successions of thought swifter than lightning flashes, and instead of the audible rap at the
right thought, there may be internal signals known
only to the heart; and signals and selections may
mingle and alternate so rapidly and continuously
that inspired action, though really compound, may

seem to be simple and merely spontaneous ; but after all these allowances for variations in details, I think it will be found that even such complex phenomena as speaking in unknown tongues, are reducible to the general principles of *selection by signals*.

"During twenty-five years of discipline in sexual matters the members of the Community have learned a great deal about the way to live out these principles practically. No doubt much of our experience would be both interesting and profitable to the thousands who are studying social problems, if it could be plainly and faithfully told. It will be hard for people to imagine the amount of milling and refining a person has to undergo before he or she is willing to submit the planning of their social and sexual affairs to the good spirit, even after they see the way to do it. That is about the last thing one is willing to yield. Yet real Communism is impossible without it. We shall be willing on our part to publish more of our experience, including personal temptations and victories, whenever there is a genuine demand for it from honest students of Communism.

"Some weeks ago Mr. Noyes wrote out, for the benefit of the younger generation in the Community, the story of his first stepping over the marriage rules. It is rather sensational, but it shows what earnestness and faithfulness in obedience to his 'control' Mr. Noyes had acquired before he was allowed any liberties outside of marriage. And it may be appropriate and useful, in these times of 'awful disclosures,' to show how such passional complications as those which brought about the terrible Beecher-Tilton scandal might have been harmonious and innocent. Readers of the *Circular* will understand what follows all the better for having read Mr. Cragin's 'Story of a Life.' Mr. Noyes gives his story under the title, 'My First Transaction in Sexual Freedom.' The germ of our social theory was developed in *The Battle-Axe* letter, and dates back to 1836–7. But the first practical step on that theory was not taken till 1846. During the intervening years we had formed a little church at Putney, and that church had gradually grown into Communism of all interests, except in the sexual department. We were theoretically prepared for the final step in Communism, but waited for orders. We had worked out the problem of Male Continence, and criticism had become an established institution among us.

"'In the Spring of 1846 I saw many reasons which I cannot now detail, for thinking that the time had come to take the final step out of marriage. I and my wife and Mr. C. and his wife were the leading couples in the Community as it then existed. I was deeply in love with Mrs. C. and she with me; as also was Mr. C. with Mrs. N. and she with him. Thus, so far as the affections were concerned, we stood 'four hands round,' and this was well understood and approved among us. This was the situation in the month of May, 1846.

"'Mrs. C. and I sometimes took pleasant walks with each other, and one evening, in the course of a stroll, we sat on a rock by the roadside in a lonely place and talked. All the circumstances seemed to invite advance in freedom, and, yielding to the impulse upon me, I took some of the liberties which usually precede sexual intercourse. The pleasure was exquisite and mutual, and the temptation to go further was tremendous. But at this point came serious thoughts. I stopped, and, in my way, 'called the alphabet.' I said to myself, *I will not steal!* I revolved in my mind as before God what to do, and when I thought of going home for confession and consultation with those who had rights in the case, I got a signal, *i. e.*, my 'control' signified to me in a sure way, that that was the true thing to do. After a moment we arose and went toward home. On the way we stopped once and took the liberty of embracing, and Mrs. C. distinctly gave me to understand that she was ready for the full consummation. I said, '*No, I am going home to report what we have done.*'' On reaching Mr. C.'s house, I called a meeting of the four, related our doings, and offered the transaction for criticism. A searching talk ensued ; Mr. C. at first was tempted to think that I was following in the footsteps of the man who had given him so much trouble years before ; but he soon recognized the difference between my course and that of his old enemy, and finally gave judgment of approval. My wife promptly

and entirely sanctioned our proceeding. The up-
shot of the conference was, that we gave each other
full liberty all round, and so entered into complex
marriage in the quartet form. The last part of the
interview was as amicable and happy as a wedding,
and a full consummation soon followed.

"The interesting point of my story is that in that
first venture I got safely past the awful temptation
to secrecy, and kept a good conscience for myself
and for Mrs. C., by consulting the invisibles and
obeying their signals. And that first venture has
been the germ and model of much of our subse-
quent experience in sexual freedom.'"

Can the reader discover in the above anything
which partakés of a "heavenly" origin, or, indeed,
anything likely to improve the morals of not over-
virtuous humanity? Does it not resemble more the
emanations of one who could not find, outside of a
well-filled harem, the gratification of a very low
order of animal passion? Think of the debasing
influence a doctrine must exert which has for its sole
end and aim the unrestrained indulgence of lust,
while it seeks to escape the responsibilities of such
indulgence by adopting "male continence," a principle which is blasphemously claimed to be of
divine inspiration!

Then, from this reasoning there is nothing sinful
in committing adultery, if you but get past the
"awful temptation to secresy." This will be news
to many who have placed their faith in Bible doc-

trines, and who have reverenced the commandment, "Thou shalt not commit adultery." As there is no "secresy" in the conducting of houses of prostitution, why, then, does not this rule apply to them? The vagueness of such philosophy is scarcely worthy of comment, and we opine that the precedent established by Noyes in the case of Mrs. Cragin would be a very dangerous one to follow, except, forsooth, in such families as the one presided over by the very amiable and devout Dr. Cragin. Instead of a "full consummation" following most cases, there would very likely follow a funeral, in which the violator of both law and decency would be an interested party.

Were anything needed to explain the character of the persons who organized Oneida Community, it is furnished in the sentence, "A searching talk ensued; Mr. C. at first was tempted to think that I was following in the footsteps of *the man who had given him so much trouble years before*," showing that Mrs. Cragin's character was not above reproach prior to her entering into "complex marriage" in the quartet form. What the "difference" was which Cragin saw between the course of Noyes in the invasion of the sanctity of his domestic life and that of his "old enemy," we are entirely at a loss to conjecture, but the supposition is that there was a general "swapping off," in which, from the report, Cragin could have nothing to lose from a moral view of the case.

CHAPTER IV.

How Interviewers are Received—M. M. Pomeroy's Interview—A Persistent Effort to
make them Unload.

Nothing is more dreaded by the Communists than
the "ubiquitous interviewer" of the press.   They
stand in constant fear of being "written up" by
some argus-eyed reporter, who, when he has given
the "wordly" side of their progress as a community, generally serves them up a broadside of invective on their morals (?) and religion.   No article
within the last decade has caused such a *furore* as
the one which appeared in *Pomeroy's Democrat*, of
New York City, about four years since, written by
the inimitable "Brick" himself.   As a specimen of
masterly reporting we give a small portion of it a
place here.   Although Mr. Pomeroy was less
favored in the "romantic" of his subject than Charles
Reade in his "James Lambert," in point of persistent effort we think it will bear something more
than a favorable comparison.

After speaking of their grounds, buildings, industries, &c., he proceeds to the subject which brought
him thither, after the following racy style :

A large building resembling a prison, asylum,

large school, or something of that sort, where a large amount of brick, stone, wood and iron was piled together under the eye and management of a competent architect, indicated to us where the Community resided. Driving through an open gate, into a large yard, in front of a long and rather handsome building capable of accommodating several hundred persons, we pulled rein at the porch where a couple of gentlemen were standing, as if awaiting our arrival, when the following conversation ensued, which we will give as it occurred, that our readers may better understand the questions asked, the answers given, and the principles, habits, and religion of the people here dwelling.

"Good morning, gentlemen."

"Good morning."

"This is Mr. Pomeroy, I presume," spake an elderly, smart, intelligent, clear-headed looking gentleman, about fifty years of age.

"Yes, sir."

"Editor of *Pomeroy's Democrat* and other papers east and west?"

"Yes, sir."

"Well, sir, you are very welcome; come in with your friends—your horses will be cared for. You are very welcome to the Community—walk in; you will find it comfortable inside."

"Thank you," and entering through the door held open for us, we were shown into a large reception room capable of holding seventy-five or an

ONEIDA COMMUNITY.—QUADRANGLE.

hundred persons. Here we found everything very neat and attractive. The room was large, well ventilated, and comfortably warmed.

The furniture was very fine and abundant, the room handsomely carpeted, and many pictures adorned the walls. We were introduced to three or four of the brothers or members of the Community, finding them all fine-looking, intelligent, pleasant-faced gentlemen. As we entered, an elderly, pleasant-faced lady, attired in what might be considered an improvement on the Bloomer costume, arose, was introduced as Mrs. Noyes, and immediately after left the room. We, with our friends, in accompany with the managing men of the association, then resumed our conversation as follows:

"Well, gentlemen, you seem to be very comfortable here; quite in contrast with the winter air, cold, and snow without. And you have a very pleasant room."

"Yes; we aim to have things comfortable here, and believe we succeed."

"Well, that's encouraging, for a life without comforts is no life at all, in the correct acceptation of the term."

"That is true. He who does not live comfortably cannot be said to enjoy enough of this life to make it worth while staying here."

"We have heard considerable concerning your society—hear your Community very highly spoken of. You have the reputation of minding your own business, living happily, prospering in your worldly affairs, and we have made a visit here for the purpose of inquiring into these things, with a view to imparting information to the public through the columns of the *Democrat.* This, gentlemen, is the object of our visit, and if you are disposed to answer, we should like to ask you a great many questions."

" We have nothing here but what we are willing everybody should know. Any questions you ask we will try and answer to the best of our ability, presuming, of course, you will ask nothing we should not answer."

"No, sir, we shall ask nothing we do not wish to know—nothing for the purpose of gratifying prurient curiosity, but to obtain information concerning your peculiar beliefs, your habits, your mode of life, why you live as you do, what advantages such a life presents, &c., &c."

"'Those questions are easily answered. All you have to do is to read our *Circular*, or the late work of Mr. Noyes, which will give you the desired information."

" We understand this book and *Circular* arrangement quite well ; they treat of abstract matters, of the great idea and principles, but do not come down to that detail which is of interest in proportion as it lets light in upon the daily life, walk, and conversation of those interested."

" Well, you will find all you wish to know concerning our life and habits in the *Circular*—everything you wish to know concerning our religious belief, &c., in the book Mr. Noyes has written, called the 'History of American Socialisms.' That book is more filled with information than any conversation could be."

"We have no doubt the book is very full, but books do not tell everything. We have had some experience as editor of a newspaper, and know that there are many things in life an editor writes of, giving information and many things coming to his knowledge of which he does not write, and it is of these things we would inquire."

"Well, it is right enough to inquire, but it seems as though all information could be obtained from our published works, which we will gladly place in your hands, and we will show you through our establishment and let you see how we live, &c.

"We are much obliged for all this, but we want to get right down to the kernel of this arrangement. In the first place, please tell us is your Community here established for the purpose of profit to individuals, or in accordance with some peculiar religious idea or belief? In fact, what is your grand *hard-pan*, on which you base your life and operations ?"

"Well, sir, we believe in God as the power of all good ; as a being of love and justice. We believe in Christ, His Son, and in so living as to be acceptable to Him when we shall be called to leave this earth."

" Then your whole mode of life is based upon a
religious belief ?"

" Yes, sir."

" And whatever you do is in conformity with your
interpretation of God's commands ?"

" Yes, sir."

" Your great aim is to live a life in consonance
with the teachings of the Almighty and the teachings of His Son, Jesus Christ ?"

" Yes, sir."

" Well, there we shall agree with you. We have
no quarrel to make upon this point. But there are
many things about your mode of life we do not like.
To be frank with you, we do not admire your system
of living together like roosters and pullets, for it is
antagonistic to our ideas of love, refinement, Chris-
tianity, and that perfection of friendship without
which there can be no real happiness in the world.
We have been educated to believe in a singleness of
purpose to a great extent, and this singleness of
love. Certainly we should not care to share the
most precious of all our gifts with any man. Not
that love is selfish, but somehow or other there is a
blessed satisfaction for a man to know that what he
has—that is, of his heart—belongs to him as he
belongs to it, without any partnership. This is
where you hold to one belief and we to another."

" All these things are explained in our works.
We refer you to them. You will see why we do
these things, and how. The results are before you.

By our works we are willing to stand, as you, doubtless, are by yours."

"Certainly. So far so good. By the works of a man we judge him and his life. We see that you are successful here. In riding along we have had pointed out to us your extensive domain, your fields under fine cultivation, your elegant buildings, your evident wealth. We meet you here as gentlemen of intellect, refinement, education, wide between the eyes, and very liberal as to ideas. But to be plain, we do not take any stock in your peculiar belief. You have everything in common. What belongs to one belongs to all. The woman one man loves all love. The woman one man caresses all caress. You live here with no singleness of purpose, so far as this life is concerned. This is more revolting than otherwise to us, and it is of this we would inquire."

"Well, our books will tell you everything. We will show you through our establishment, and convince you, if possible."

"Never mind the books at present. We will get to this theory by-and-by. We believe in a singleness of purpose to a great extent; in a singleness of love, thereby concentrating and making the same stronger, that men may be happier here, and, by that happiness, better fitted for happiness hereafter. This, we believe is in accordance with the popular and generally accepted belief. What is your idea?"

"Well, our singleness of purpose, as you call it,

is devoted exclusively to Christ. We look to Him, and him only, as the author of love and hope of our salvation. And we are earnest in our singleness of purpose to him; we look upon all as belonging to Him, upon all members of one family as brothers and sisters—feeling that everything is in common, made so by that perfect love which comes to us from this Higher Power and which you or the world cannot understand till you have been educated as we have been."

" Then you have no jealousies and rivalries, feelings of enmity, one toward another, as in communities outside?"

"No; not to an extent that gives us any trouble."

"Well, this is singular."

" Yes, it would appear singular to those not agreeing with the educated as we have been, not thinking as we do."

"Have you a wife?"

"No, sir, my wife died several years ago—that is the one you would call wife. She died soon after my coming here."

"Do you often feel the want of some one person, above all others, to whom you can talk? Some person you can caress, and who would caress you; whose life would seem to run of its own accord in with yours, and yours with hers? Some hand of more than ordinary sympathy? Some person whose touch has that electricity which fills a man with love and feelings indescribable? Some one person dearer

than all the world to you? Do you not often feel
this want; this need of something which will relieve
your thoughts of the cares of the world, and give
you strength, through love and perfection of friend-
ship, to make you strong for the battles of life."

"No; not as you rather pointedly put the question. We are wedded to Christ as you would be
wedded to the object of your heart's admiration, as
you feelingly express it. We go directly to the
Saviour for all this comfort that you would seek
from earthly persons."

"Well, do you not sometimes feel the need of a
sympathy, a love, a friendship?"

"Oh, certainly, we feel that, and we find it here.
We are all brothers and sisters; all alike before
God, before Christ, in belief and sentiment. Our
love for each other is perfect. We find sympathy
everywhere in our community. Each sympathizes
with the other, each loves the other with that perfect love which comes from perfect belief."

"Then your belief is perfect? By that you have
faith—full faith that you are right, doing right, living right, and so living as to insure to you crowns
of happiness, power, &c., in the future?"

"Yes, we have full faith. Our faith comes from
perfect love. That perfect love comes to us from a
singleness of devotion to Christ."

"Tell us, if you please, about your mode of life
here."

"We live here much as other people do. We

eat, drink and sleep. We live together in friend-ship, each one minding his own business and attend-ing to his or her duties. And we think we enjoy ourselves here as well, if not better, than persons outside.''

"But your living together so in common is what we cannot understand. The Bible tells us it is not good for man to be alone.''

"But, we are not alone. We are about evenly divided as to men and women, male and female, brothers and sisters.''

"We mean that it is not good for man to live without the loving care of some woman ; as it is not right for woman to live without the care and pro-tection of some man, loved by her, and who loves her above all others.''

"Well, that is where you believe one thing, and we another. You believe in this singleness of pur-pose and devotion to one woman ; but we, with more liberality and love of Christ in our hearts, love as He commands us, and we love each other alike.

"That is exceedingly liberal—to say the least. We can understand how one can love his brother as himself, but when it comes to sharing the object of his heart's adoration with a brother, or permitting that brother to kiss, caress, and be as intimate with his wife or the woman he loves—that's where you have us.''

"If you understood our religion, and had been

converted to our belief, you would think differently ; you would understand all this."

"We should have to understand a great deal, and be greatly altered from our present make-up."

"Through God and His love all things are possible."

"We don't believe it possible for God to make us love a partnership of that kind ! We don't go a cent on partners as a general thing. We want no bed for three to sleep in—except in case of rare emergency where one is caught out in a storm.

"Oh, if you thought as we do you would think differently !"

"Quite likely ! But we can't see how you can share all these blessings of life with each other as you do. There is something beyond our comprehension. Now, if we love a woman we don't want any one else to have anything to do with her. To tell the truth, we do love a woman very dearly. A thousand times when at work we would like to have the privilege of resting with her and by her, caressing her and being caressed, looking into her eyes, taking her hands in ours, feeling that our hearts were growing together for the strengthening of the love which passeth the understanding of man. We don't want anybody else round her."

"Now, you are all pretty good-looking here ; wide between the eyes, good, kind, and intelligent. But if we should see any one of you making love to our darling, squeezing her hand, kissing her, and, above all things, occupying the same room and couch with her, somebody would have a *busted head,* sure !"

"Well, that is because you are more devoted to her than to Christ. Your singleness of purpose is directed to the one you love best, or the object which most engrosses your attention. Ours is taken up by the great source of all love."

"Yes, certainly ; but tell us something about how you get along with this thing. We can't understand it. You live here in common. What do you do for a wife ? There are times when you must have some one to be with you. There are children here—evidences that you have not forgotten that portion of the Bible which says: 'Multiply and replenish the earth.' How do you manage this if you have no wives ?"

"Oh, well—why, that is all easy enough with us. This is the result of our education, our—our—our determination to be guided by intellect rather than passion."

"We'll suppose a case. To get at what we want, suppose that we have just arrived here as a member of your society. Now, you men do not look like persons who would like to live hermits, alone all your days, like Robinson Crusoe, with no one around except Man Friday. Life to us without a companionship of woman would be just no life at all—as a season without sunshine would be very dull, gloomy and irksome. Suppose we come to you as one of you and say, 'Gentlemen here we are.' "

"Well, then, we should say you are here. You would do as we do."

"Yes, but we want somebody to sew on shirt-buttons, darn our stockings, fix our garters, do a little work with needle and thread once in a while. Sometimes to put camphor, cologne, bay-rum, and Florida water on our head when it aches, as it often does from overwork. To fix up our hair and handkerchiefs, to hold our head in her lap, and tell us once in a while, in a whisper, so that no one else would understand it, that she loved us. Not merely for the sake of having these things done, but to know that among all of God's millions there was some *one*, some earnest, true, loving, virtuous woman, who was ours to live for, work for, and make happy—in short, a wife, as the word is used by the public at large."

"We have all of that. Every one of us has a woman to take care of his things, to sew on buttons, put his room in order, and camphor on his head, as you say, to bring his clothes from the laundry, and to whom he looks for all those little attentions which men and women should bestow upon each other."

"Then each one of you persons has what you would call a wife, the same as us persons not belonging to your community have, who are married and raising families?"

"We have no wives here. We know nothing of marriage as you define the word. We are all married men and women ; altogether in one family ; no partiality being shown to this one or that one."

"Do you mean to tell me that none of you men are married ? That you have no wives in the wifely acceptation of the term ?"

"We have no wives, as you call them. We call them 'mothers,' here. I have no wife, but I have a 'mother.' She takes care of my room, and does all this little fine work, you speak of—talks with me, and I with her when the time comes."

"Well, who is she ? What is her name ? What do you call her ?

"We call her 'mother.' She is a young woman, about twenty-four years of age, and she is to me what one's wife would be to him."

"These other gentlemen here are in the same fix, are they ? Each one with an object of attachment, so to speak ; inside, of course, of your lines of love to Christ ?"

"Yes, each one of us is so situated. Now, this gentleman here [pointing to one on his right] has two daughters in the Community. One of these daughters acts as his 'mother !' "

"What is that ? Do you say that man's daughter is his mother ? Rather singular !"

"He has two daughters. One of them is his 'mother,' so-called, who takes care of his clothing,

&c. The other daughter is the 'mother' of another of our brethren.''

"Well, that is reducing the thing down to about as fine a point as we ever heard of. Almost any man ought to be satisfied with a religion like that. But, tell us further. You, of course, in selecting your 'mother,' as you call her—wife, as we call her —are guided by more than an indiscriminate laying on of hands upon the first woman that comes along? Surely your love, or sympathy, or affection, or affinity, whatever you may call it—would not cause every female to look, and act, and feel, and be, and perform, &c., the same to you as one which might find more than ordinary favor in your eyes?''

"Oh, we have our regulations here. Of course, we do not take to our rooms those who would be disagreeable to us from any cause, such as sickness, &c.''

"Then, it seems to us, your love for each other is not so perfect as it might be, when it comes to the women part of the question. You love all men here alike, but you seem to have a partiality for women, else why do you select each one of you a woman whom you call 'mother' to look to and be with, &c., when comes the hour for the tasting of certain fruits, &c. Now, here is where the row would commence were we a member of this institution. If we were here we should feel like selecting some one that would just suit us, providing there was somebody who would be suited with us, and then if we caught any of the people around here making a visit late in the evening, or playing 'who's been here since I've been gone,' somebody would walk off with a bullet-hole in them. We should not allow any of that interference with our especial preserves. And yet you people claim that you do not live lives of constancy to one?"

"Oh, no; our love for each other is so perfect that we do not consider that we wrong a brother in honoring or conferring happiness or pleasure upon a woman who may be wifely to him, as you use the term."

"Well, this is about the mellowest liberality we ever heard of. Do you allow the same privileges to outsiders, newspaper men, etc., that come here?"

"By no means! None but those of our family partake of the family property."

"Ah, we see; that is very good. How do you regulate these things?"

"Oh, they regulate themselves easy enough."

"Suppose one of your women here, one of your 'mothers,' or whatever you may call them, becomes the parent of four children, does it follow that one man is the father of the four, according to your rules, religion, etc.?"

"By no means. A woman is not obliged to have any one man as the father of her children."

"Then you know nothing here of being true to each other—that is, living a life of constancy, man to woman, and woman to man?"

"Not as you use the word, but as we do. For in loving one another, and conferring happiness upon each other, we believe we are true to each other."

"Then you would not consider it wrong, upon returning to your room at night, to find a brother occupying your place in your sleeping apartment, with the one you expected to repose with from early night till dewy morn."

"No; we should not consider any wrong was being done. But these mistakes, as you might call them, do not occur."

"Suppose we desired to join your society. Take it for granted that we have become a convert to your ideas, and your belief in this concentration of thought, mind, belief, and everything else to Christ, paying no attention to outside interference or inside feelings; grant that we have applied to you for admission to this association; suppose that we have signified our willingness to join, in fact our anxiety to join, and have said to you, gentlemen, our age is so many years, our name is as it is, our habits so and so, our financial wealth so much; we now wish to become a member of your community; what do you do then?"

"Well, we should talk of this matter in our meetings for criticism; would discuss the case, and decide whether it would be advisable or not to admit you as a member.

"The question would be referred to a committee, whose report would be considered as binding, unless some one should make serious objection. If you were considered a fit person to belong, you would be notified that you could come, and we should expect you to conform to our wishes and regulations, but should you at any time wish to leave you could do so."

"Suppose we should bring fifty thousand dollars in cash, a trunkful of clothes, and our personal body to you—remain a year, more or less, then wish to depart ?"

"No one would hinder you. If you did not wish to stay you could go, for we do not want any discontented persons with us. The money you brought to the concern would be paid back to you without interest, for we should consider that in caring for you, &c., &c., we had given you interest upon your money ; and should not be under any obligations to pay you any salary or wages."

" Well, that would be all right. Take it for granted that we have been elected, and have come here. We are by some vehicle or other brought from the depot to your door. We come in; set down our valise, trunk, band-box, chest of clothes, kit of tools, &c., &c., and say 'Good morning, eminent gentlemen, here we are, ready for anything and everything. Please consider us as one of the Oneida Community, a brother duly elected, entitled to all the rights, privileges, benefits, immunities, and communities.' Then what ?"

" Well, a committee of members would take your

ONEIDA COMMUNITY.—EAST FRONT.

case under consideration. They would know and understand your habits, abilities, capacities, &c., and give you a position or something to do in accordance with your adaptation."

"Yes; but we should want a little room, a little 'think-shop'—some place we could call our own, where we could close the doors, sit back in our chair, stretch out the arms, think how we would do work, &c.—some place where we could rest and feel as though we had within those four walls a little place or spot where persons could not enter unless invited. Could we have such a place here ?"

"Certainly. The committee would give you a room—a 'think-shop,' as you call it, and fit it up in accordance with your worth and standing, your ability, your material tastes or desires. We should endeavor to make you just as much at home as we feel. And in proportion to your means, your capacity, your ability to plan and to aid, in such degree would be given you prominence, position, &c."

"Well, that is all right. Now a little further. After being here awhile we discover that it is not well for man to dwell alone, and want some—some —some—woman ! No matter what we want her for, whether it is a 'mother' to sew on shirt-buttons, bathe our head, or what not. How are we to get one ? Do we stand in the hall, and whenever a good-looking, neat, tasty, sweet, attractive, &c., &c., woman, just the one to be a companion to a rather warm-blooded, ambitious, lively sort of delegate, comes along, do we tip her the wink, call her up into a corner, introduce ourself and say, ' Mariar Jane, the number of our room is 743 ; come in ; we will be there with a tallow candle turned down low, and a memorandum book.' "

" Not exactly."

" Well, then, how are we to arrange this matter ? Of course, you would not expect a full-fledged member, and rooster of high repute, so to speak, to live like a hermit without her ? "

" Certainly not."

" How, then, are we to go to work to find some-body to be our ' mother ? ' Suppose we get our eye upon one that just suits us, and discover that she is your ' mother,' or another gentleman's ' mother,' and when we invite her to come around to 743, she says, ' Shoo fly ! excuse me ; I am engaged for this evening ? ' That's what we want to know—how you fix this thing ? "

" Well—the love of Christ so fills our hearts that we do not want what another has ; and if we did want it, it is all right that we should have it."

" All right ! Then the best man wins here. The livliest turkey catches the most grasshoppers."

" No ; *not* exactly that way. We don't have any lively turkeys here. That is not our business."

" Of course not ; but how is this thing fixed ? That's what we want to know. Suppose we want somebody to do all this little fine hand work, and on looking around find that partners have been taken before us, then must we scoot around from door to door trying to find one not locked, dodge in, say 'Good morning, Jane, just called in to make a friendly visit,' &c., and go on, &c., &c.-ing in that way?"

"No. But you are asking peculiar questions. We never have had such funny questions put to us before. Our books tell all about these things."

"Books do not tell about this, and this is just what we want to know. If you don't see fit to answer us, all right. Don't consider us impertinent, but we came here for information, and we want information upon this very point, for it is what no one can tell us. If you do not see fit to answer, why, of course, we cannot obtain the information, and must draw our own conclusions. But we want to know all about it. Some of these days we may become disgusted with the way things are conducted in this world, and apply for admission here, giving you an opportunity to black-ball or admit us as you see fit. Knowing something about how things are conducted outside, we would know how they are managed here; then we can judge which is best."

"Well, sir, should you come here a committee would consider all these questions, &c., and after you had become acquainted and expressed a desire to have as your companion or 'mother' a certain woman, this committee would ask her if she had any objections, &c. You would be brought together, and if your affinity, so to speak, ran to each other, why, it would be all right!"

"Then this matter is not left to the choice of the man and woman themselves?"

"No; a third party settles these questions. The ones interested do not speak to each on these matters at all."

"Well, that's a pretty way to make love! Something as they do in Armenia, where wives are sold and not suffered to show their faces to their husbands till they have been married a year. We hardly think we should enjoy this plan, for there is nothing more pleasant than courtship, except it is enjoying the fruit of that courtship."

"Our association so regulates these matters that all are satisfied."

"Suppose your association should see fit to give us—a warm-blooded, vigorous delegate—should apportion to us as our part of the profits of this association, a venerable dame, old enough to be our grandmother? Suppose she was the only one of all the flock here that would like us well enough to permit certain familiarities which are evidently not unfashionable here, and that we should have a *hankering* for somebody else, and at last, that somebody else should reciprocate our hankering? Would it then be necessary for us to dodge around slyly to obtain interviews whereby and wherefore certain objects might be accomplished, providing such was our desire. or would it be considered all right to boldly enter in upon and take possession of? In other words, would the brother more immediately interested be angry upon finding a stray rabbit in his trap?"

"Oh, no; this is all in accordance with that great love. Here no brother can wrong a brother by being familiar with any of the sisters. Nor does a sister wrong any brother by being familiar with another. There are times and places, and opportunities continually presenting themselves, and those who see fit to love, caress, show affection, &c., have no one to interfere with them."

"That's all right. We are glad to hear you are so liberal. Now, suppose a woman becomes the mother of a child, whose name does the child bear?"

"Why, the father's name, of course."

"But suppose there should be some little doubt in the mind of the woman as to who was the father of the child?"

"Oh, there is an old saying that a woman generally knows who is the father of her baby."

"Yes—just so. But you tell us that you are devoted only to each other; that you men have nothing to do with the people outside—that is, except in the line of business. In other words, that no children outside in this neighborhood bear any striking resemblance to members of the Oneida Community?"

"No; we do not allow anything of that kind. In

fact, we have no desire to prove recreant to our duty," &c.

"That is right; that's right! We do not see that there would be much need of traveling a great way for comforts beyond the limits of your Community. You have children here, of course? Who takes care of them? Are they considered children of individuals or children of the Community?"

"They are children of individuals and of the Community. Each one is interested in the welfare of the other. They are our children, supported by the Community, educated and cared for; of course bearing the name of the father."

" Suppose a man and woman here thrown together became attached to each other, as they do outside of this Community. After being together more or less they think they are indispensable to each other's happiness. Suppose they become heretical—so to speak—the man thinks he loves that woman more than any and all others—and the woman in returning this affection for him, learning, as women will if they are good and virtuous, to look with a certain degree of indifference or loathing upon the attention of others. And suppose the man becomes absorbed in his love for this one woman, and that the woman is only happy when with that man. Suppose these two find their lives running into each other, thinking alike, desiring alike, having the same passions, the same warmth of blood and generosity of touch and sentiment—a disposition to live for, by, of, and unto each other. Do you allow this?"

"Well—in our evening meetings, when we all assemble as a family, we should criticise their conduct, point to the evil of their ways, question the genuineness of their religion ; and if they persisted in living in violation of our faith, drawing themselves so closely together as to attract the attention of the Community, thinking more of each other and the gratification of their love, desires, passions, &c., than of Christ, we should say to them they had better go, for they were not of us—and we should not want them with us, harmony being necessary to complete success."

"Then you have no constancy here other than your religion. Everything is subservient to that ? You put up goods, manufacture certain articles, selling them to the best advantage, and you enjoy yourselves, when comes the hour of relaxation, as inclination suggests or dictates ?"

"Yes, we live here as brothers and sisters—all alike. What belongs to one belongs to all. As brothers and sisters think it no harm to kiss each other promiscuously, so do we think it no harm nor sin to confer happiness whenever, wherever, and by whatever means we can to those of our own Community. And the women consider that we are doing them honor in showing them the attentions you hint at and openly speak of."

"Do you room apart—the men here and women there—or domicile together ?"

"Oh, that is as it happens. Some of the women

sleep in this part of the house, and some in that ; some of the men here, and some there. We have our rooms, of course, but all are cared for alike— and if one man happens to be found in another man's room, or *vice versa*, there are no hard feelings ; it is all right."

"We presume you have keys upon the door, so that a man would not be disturbed in his devotions ? And, of course, you would not tolerate the break- ing of locks ?"

"Yes, our doors have locks."

CHAPTER V.

"MALE CONTINENCE"—SCIENTIFIC PRINCIPLES FOR THE GRATIFICATION OF LUST — SCIENTIFIC PROPAGATION, &c.

To prove the great (?) benefit to humanity of the discovery of "male continence," Noyes has published a pamphlet on the subject, a portion of which we had intended to reproduce in this work, and had gone so far as to copy a paragraph or two for publication. Upon more mature deliberation, and in view of its licentious character, we concluded to submit the portion selected to an attorney for legal advice, and he unequivocally declared that it would be an open and flagrant violation of statute law to reproduce it. Take into consideration the fact that the extract above referred to was as decent as could well be chosen in elucidating the subject of "male continence," and the reader may get a faint idea of the nastiness of Noyes' work as a whole. Under this legal advice we eliminated the most obnoxious sentences, and give the following excerpt, which may serve our purpose as well; but the seeker after obscene literature need extend his searches no further than Oneida Community for the fullest satisfaction of his desires.

Below is the all important discovery which Noyes has handed down to his followers as an important plank in the Communistic platform :

"Experimenters in the art of controlling propagation may be reduced in principle to three classes, viz. :

"1. Those that seek to prevent the intercourse of the sexes.

"2. Those that seek to prevent the natural effects of the propagative act.

"3. Those that seek to destroy the living results of the propagative act.

"Our theory of 'male continence' consists in analyzing sexual intercourse, recognizing in it two distinct acts, the social and the propagative, which can be separated practically, and affirming that it is best, not only with reference to remote prudential considerations, but for immediate pleasure, that a man should content himself with the social act, except when he intends procreation.

"Let us now see if this scheme belongs to any of the three classes I mentioned. 1. It does not seek to prevent the intercourse of the sexes, but rather gives them more freedom by removing danger of undesired consequences. 2. It does not seek to prevent the natural *effects* of the propagative act, but to prevent the propagative act itself, except when it is intended to be effectual. 3. Of course it does not seek to destroy the living *results* of the propagative act, but provides that impregnation and child-bearing shall be voluntary, and of course desired.

"And now, to speak affirmatively, the exact thing that our theory does propose, is to take that same power of moral restraint and self-control, which * * * * * * * * all considerate men use in one way or another to limit propagation, and instead of applying it, as they do, to the prevention of the intercourse of the sexes, to introduce it at another stage of the proceedings, viz., *after* the sexes have come together in social effusion, and *before* they have reached the propagative crisis ; thus allowing them all and more than all the ordinary freedom of love (since the crisis always interrupts the romance), and at the same time avoiding undesired procreation and all other evils incident to male incontinence. This is our fourth way, and we think it the better way."

Noyes said, in 1842, alluding to the publication of the *Battle-Axe* Letter: "From that time I have never faltered in my purpose of publishing on the house-tops the truths contained in that letter." How well he has performed his self-imposed task, the foregoing extracts but too fully testify. As the writer in the *Circular* remarks, they are "*somewhat* sensational," but they are not given place in this book for the purpose of pandering to lust nor to satisfy prurient curiosity. To show to what depths of animal degradation these people are capable of descending, it will only be necessary to give one more

sample from their organ. This we find in the issue
of November 7, 1870, which is almost entirely devoted to the social arrangements of the Community,
at least so far as they desire to have them known,
and they are bad enough. In reviewing and com-
paring the sanitary condition of the Community
with the outside world, Dr. T. R. Noyes, a son (?)
of the head of Perfectionism, says: "Several years
ago, in consequence of doubts thrown upon our system by prominent medical men, who said that our
limitation of propagation is not due to voluntary
control, because male continence will certainly produce impotence in men and sterility in women, *we
tested the virile condition of the men by a general
microscopical examination of semen*, showing that,
as far as abundant and active zoösperms are evidence, we have retained our natural powers in nearly
every case, including those up to sixty-five or sev-
enty years of age. The question has been set at
rest *as regards our women* by late movements in the
direction of systematic propagation. Previous to
about two and a half years ago, we refrained from
the usual rate of child-bearing for several reasons,
financial and otherwise. Since that time we have
made an attempt to produce the usual proportion of
offspring to which people in the middle classes are
able to afford judicious spiritual and moral care,
with the advantage of a liberal education. In this
attempt *twenty-four women and twenty men have
been engaged, selected from among those who have*

thoroughly practiced our social theory. The result has been the *impregnation of sixteen women* in a period of about two years, which result will compare favorably, we think, with the average fertility of ordinary married women for the same time. It is to be observed that the junction of the sexes was not, by any means, the usual continuous occupation of the same bed, as is the case among married people in common life. They did not average over four times a month, confined generally to the two weeks after the cessation of the menstrual period."

Thus, it will be seen, that whatever is done by the Communists in their sexual matters, is first apologized for by some pretext—in the interest of "science." Imagine a "general microscopical examination" of over one hundred men! It is positively too filthy for any one to contemplate, but is in perfect harmony with those who consult their "immediate" pleasure in such matters, rather than to "multiply and replenish the earth."

And now a word in regard to Communistic "scientific propagation." What has proved true in the case of an entire nation, as it were, will be very likely to hold good of a community numbering less than three hundred. They claim that their children are healthier and more intelligent than legitimate offspring, and that their system of intermingling does not deteriorate their issue. Would the results of a community which has had an existence of but twenty-seven years, prove such a fact? Not at all;

for there the relations of those selected for propagation do not vary from those who enter marriage in
ordinary life. They do not select cousins or rela-
tives of any kind for that purpose. Then, why
should not their offspring be equally intelligent?
Deterioration will not be noticeable, probably, until
three or four generations have come together, should
their institution stand that length of time. In the
cantons of Switzerland, where the marriage of first
cousins for one generation after another is of frequent occurrence, the *American Journal of Insan-
ity* says dwarfness, cretinism and idiocy are disgustingly prevalent.

Dr. J. G. Spurzheim, who is acknowledged as eminent authority upon the subject, says: "Scarcely
one among the royal families of Europe, who have
married in an in for generations, can write a page of
consecutive sound sense on any scientific, or literary,
or moral subject.

Dr. Charles Caldwell says that "one cause of
human deterioration is family marriages. It has
almost extinguished most of the royal families of
Europe, though at first they were the notables of
the land for physical strength, and force of mind
and character."

"Moses condemned it, even though he thereby
practically censured his national patriarchs; doubtless because of its palpably deteriorating effects,"
says the learned Dr. Allen.

Instances might be cited in proof of the falsity

of the doctrine of "complex marriage" which would fill an ordinary library, were they needed. The beasts of the field or farm do not bear out the assertion of its superiority even. How long would a flock of sheep, for instance, thrive under such a state of "breeding in and in?" The least scientific or observing boy would answer this question unhesitatingly against such a theory. Is it possible, then, that a small community of men and women are capable of reversing the law of animal production?

Prof. Fowler says, and the world will bear him out in the assertion, that "only those who may always *love* each other, become parents together, and rear their mutual children in honor" have any right to cohabit together, and "a reunion under other circumstances would beget only animal children." Again we quote from the same author: "Offspring constitute Nature's only ultimate end of all cohabitation. Solely to produce them was each sex, and every part and parcel of each of their sexual structures, created and adapted. This sexual institute and apparatus were not devised and executed mainly or merely to yield its participants pleasure. Its enjoyments are Nature's means, incentive, and reward for its action, not its end. The pleasures of intercourse are merely incidental, while offspring alone is primal. Therefore its possessors may not indulge in it merely for pastime, or as a luxury. God did not institute it for any such purpose. He permits its fullest enjoyment only to those who fulfill its divine, life-imparting mission ; but it is too holy to be sacrilegiously profaned to riotous luxury. * * * * Enjoy it all you like in and by carrying out its primal ends ; but you profane it to lustful purposes at your peril."

Do the members of the Oneida Community profane this divine right to lustful purposes? Let us see. In the paragraph given from their *Circular* on "scientific propagation," but *twenty-four* females were selected from over five times that number, and the time mentioned in which *sixteen* were brought to conceive, was something over *two years*. This low ratio of births to the number of adult females can only be accounted for in two ways. One is, that given by themselves—for "financial reasons." The other, and altogether the most probable one, is, they had given themselves over to riotous luxury. Their great wealth precludes the former as a sufficient reason, and Noyes' assertion that "*adultery, fornication, and incest, are not bad in themselves,* but bad because the law makes them so," would seem very good authority for the latter supposition.

The principle of "scientific propagation," it is claimed by Noyes, makes the parentage of children born in the Community a certainty, as a "herd book" is used for keeping a careful pedigree record. But this is more than nonsensical, even for a "Heavenly Association" to claim. Noyes says that in

" mongrel " society there is no incentive for keeping
a faithful record, and those that are kept, compared
with those which scientific propagation necessitates,
are mere "chalk marks," and "wholly unsuitable
to the approaching era of stirpiculture." From this
it will be seen that the Apostle of Perfectionism has
risen to that degree of security in his stronghold as
to not only be able to defy the statutes of the land,
but to "call names,"—a confidence which should
be summarily torn from him by the laws he and his
followers are daily transgressing. The proposition
that a man who has passed a long life in the basest
of prostitution will scruple at falsehood, is hardly
tenable; and in this matter of pedigree, the state-
ments of a set of libertines may well be taken with
many grains of allowance. There are few children
in Oneida Community who know any more of their
parentage than the beasts of the field. If there are
exceptions, which we doubt very much, they belong
to the class selected for scientific propagation, and
not to the common horde of that den of iniquity.

CHAPTER VI.

That Noyes was leading by the nose a hare-brained
set, is evidenced by the shrewdness which he mani-
fests in planning for the consummation of his own
lustful desires. It is a law of the Community that,
to use their own words, "it is not desirable for *two
inexperienced and unspiritual persons to rush into
fellowship with each other ;* that it is far better for
both to associate with persons of mature character
and sound sense." Noyes' application of this doctrine is, that the young and inexperienced maidens
of the Community should not be allowed to have
sexual intercourse with the young and inexperienced
males of the "family;" and accordingly, when a girl
has arrived at the age of twelve years she is handed
over to the man of "mature character," to be robbed
of her virtue. After having satiated his passions
upon her, she is turned over to the flock as one

possessed of "experience, mature character and sound sense," and ripe for fellowship with those of the lower order. There is no restraint placed upon sexual intercourse, when practiced in accordance with the inspired doctrine of "male continence." That is, "all men are *expected* to make it a *point of honor* to refrain from the propagative part of sexual connection, except when propagation is intended and provided for by due consultation with the Community and with the other party concerned." (See *Circular*, Nov. 7, 1870.) After a female comes from the hand of Noyes she is called "mother," the males of the Community being known only to each other as "brother." When a child is born, it is cared for by its mother until it is weaned, after which time it is placed with the other children, under the care of those supposed to be best adapted to its management, the mother caring for it every night until it is five years old. At this age the child is not regarded as a fit bed companion, for reasons which will very naturally force themselves upon the mind of the reader.

This brings us to the consideration of another important feature of the Community, namely, the means adopted for "pairing off" by those considered "spiritual" enough for lustful indulgences. As in all other matters, J. H. Noyes is first consulted on the subject, and then the question comes up in the "family circle" for "free criticism," or a committee is appointed to adjust matters with the

"mother," who has been coveted by the "brother."
This is the fundamental law of the institution, and
it knows no exception. So long as a woman shares
the bed of a man in the Community, she must
minister to his wants, as a wife would do in the
ordinary walks of life. When she is wanted by
another brother the same routine is gone through
with. Although it is claimed that the women are
free to reject whomsoever they choose, this is not
the case, and many of them have been subjected to
severe flogging for non-compliance with the wishes
of the men. Should this be doubted, it is only
necessary to refer to the case of Sarah Hubbard.
This woman was subjected to such brutal treatment
that her brother interposed and had the ringleaders
arrested and brought to trial, during the progress of
which one of the Community women testified that
Miss Hubbard's case was not an exceptional one,
that she herself had been forced to have connection
with *sixty different men in the brief space of* TWO
WEEKS! Yet this astounding information only pro-
voked the imposition of a nominal fine from the
dispensers of justice in Madison County.

To still further give evidence of the venal and sen-
suous nature of communistic life, we will present
some of the minor details of their "Heavenly Association." The members of the Community are
taught to entirely ignore the Sabbath, and this day
is given over to the gratification of worldly desires,
amusements. &c. Whatever of moral sensibility

they ever possessed has become blunted to such an
extent by the teachings of their crafted and villain-
ous leader as to render them but little above the
brute creation, as far as morality is concerned.
What more could be expected from a people whose
leader has declared that "public prayer is hypocriti-
cal," and who "abrogates the whole moral law as
summarily contained in the ten commandments."

As might well be inferred from the general tone of
their works, they have no secrets among them in relation to sexual commerce, and the subject is discussed
with as much freedom and very much after the manner a stock-breeder would handle the subject. Indeed, Noyes has often abjured his followers to let
their intercourse and relations be as "free as the
fowls of the barn-yard." It is but a few years since
that the men and women of this institution used to
bathe in Oneida Creek together, in open day, as nude
as when they came into the world ! But their indecent exhibitions were soon complained of by citizens
of the surrounding country, and the practice discontinued.

The members of the Community claim to have at-
tained to man's estate before the fall ; that is, they
have arrived at that degree of perfection which
knows no such thing as shame, and although they
have not advocated the "fig leaf" style of dress as
yet, they undoubtedly would adopt it were it not for
the law which compels them to do otherwise. The
following in relation to this subject is from some of

their adherents, who are outside of the fold, but who should be inside of some insane asylum or other place until their notions of decency became more exalted. It is taken from the *Community Circular* of March 8, 1875:

C. W. F., ——, Mass. " When in England I was led to think Communism practicable, but I am afraid if I should adopt it that I should go to the very extreme of radicalism. I am inclined to accept the view of the Shakers that the forbidden fruit was that of sexual intercourse, and the partaking of it (improperly) led to the covering of those organs artificially. If this be so it seems to me that a complete remedy must imply the discarding of all dress. It seems to me that in *dress* men and women reach the climax of artificiality, and the so-called ' sun cure' is an argument in favor of a ' return to nature' by discarding dress."

C. E. G. C., Bombay, India. " Do you give any practical countenance to Adamitism ? One great principle, community of women, you have adopted ; but how about going naked ? You have got rid of shame, and there seem to me to be many practical advantages in at least occasional nakedness. Please give me an answer if only to tell me that I am a fool."

The reply to these notes was quite characteristic. They did not really advocate nakedness on account of the climate being unsuited to the " primitive state." But there could be no possible harm come

from it! They have undertaken "occasional nakedness," and the temperature raised by the demands
of society for a cessation of their indecent exhibitions was so "warm" as to force them into more
becoming attire.

In regard to the "heavenly" nature of their institution, the Communists first blow hot and then cold.
They will first assert that the utmost harmony pre-
vails in the camp, and then something will occur of
a sufficiently aggravated character to excite their
ire, when the malcontent is brought to the surface,
through their organ, and handled without gloves.
In this respect they do not differ materially from
"mongrel" society in general, and the average
"ungodly" newspaper editor. But as they have a
way of reconciling the most beastly of all forms of
sexual commerce with the strictest ideas of morality,
and even *religion*, of course they will not be per-
plexed in the least to present some plausible pretext
for conduct which may seem a little strange to those
not versed in the complicated workings of "heavenly
associations."

A case in point is that of one William Mills (we
cite it as being the most remarkable of any they
have cared to divulge), which culminated, in 1864,
by "some of the brethren carefully setting Mills'
goods and person out of doors," as the *Circular* of
November 20, 1865, has it.

The cause of the rupture between Mills and the
Community grew out of the former's rejection by

the women, which he refers to in a letter to his
eldest daughter Ellen, as follows :

"You say you feel isolated because of the law I
have put you under, or because I have not felt free
to let you associate with men, in a sexual way--If
two or three weeks will Isolate you from the Community, what do you think of your Father, whose
social addresses has been spurned by almost every
woman in the Community for most 5 years."

And this spirit of jealousy, which they claim does
not exist among them, furnishes much of the inward
turmoil to which they are subject, but which is only
hinted at in the occasional published reports of
their "criticisms."

The war on Mills continued over a year, under the
heading of "The Parasite," and was conducted
throughout with the bitterest invective and lowest
ribaldry at the command of the sainted Noyes, who
seems to have been chosen to wield the cudgel. His
fitness for such a task will be disgustingly apparent
in some of the extracts which we shall reproduce.

It seems that Mills, like most men who seek such
an institution, had wrecked his own family by his
venality before they were admitted to membership,
as the following testimony of his divorced wife
shows. It is copied from the *Circular* of Jan. 16,
1865 :

"When his daughter Sarah was fourteen years
old Mr. Mills got in with the Spiritualists and had
Sarah and Ellen for his mediums ; he used to shut

them up in a room, put them into the transic state,
and then question them. At this time he put Sarah
at the head of the family, and forbade Mrs. Mills
to do anything about the house. Sarah was allowed
to disobey her and be saucy to her, and so were all
the children. Mr. Mills told Sarah if her mother
struck her, he would strike her mother. Mrs. Mills
was jealous of the intimacy between Mr. Mills and
Sarah, suspecting them even of incest, as also the
neighbors did and do to this day; though Mrs.
Mills does not really think now there was anything
so bad, as Sarah does not confess it. One day Mr.
Mills had one of the girls in a room alone, and Mrs.
Mills peeped through the key-hole and saw her
stretched on a table in a pretended trance. Mr.
Mills asked her if her mother had reported to the
neighbors any of her suspicions about him and
Sarah. The medium said, "Yes.' 'Who to?' 'To
Mrs. F——.' Mrs. Mills only stopped to hear this
when she burst into the room and pulled the girl to
her feet and gave her a violent shaking, saying, ' I
wont have such lies told in the house.' Mr. Mills
first begged the spirits not be offended at this inter-
ruption, and then threatened Mrs. Mills' life, told her
he would make the house too hot for her, and advised
her to escape before he got too mad. She went soon
after and found a new home ; and subsequently sued
for a divorce, and obtained it by swearing that she
was in fear of her life."

After Mills' forcible ejection from the Community

he sought to recover by law what he had contributed
on becoming one of the "family," and this fact
seems to have been the animus which carried on the
war for so long a time waged with unabated nastiness. The defense of the Community, through
Noyes, was, that Mills had attempted to *force* the
women. It appears that his personal attractions
were the chief cause of his bad success with the
females, as he is dubbed the "apostle of ugliness"
in some of the articles written against him. The bad
luck which Mills encountered in his advances is best
told in his letters, which were published in the issue
of Jan. 9, 1865. They are unique specimens.

Oneida Community N. Y. Jan 1. 1863.

Mrs Miller—Dear Sister—I have felt for a year
that sometime I would open my heart to you and
tell you how I have felt towards you and what experience I have had in connection with it, I have
of late been discontented, and have thought of send-
ing for Charles and Ellen [over whom he had no
lawful control,] and having all the children removed from the Community I know this would be a
dreadful stroke on the Community, but I have sub-
mitted my condition and circumstances to God the
best way I know how, and if God cannot sustain
me in the Community there is no other alterity left
me but to leave, And after I have made up my
mind to leave believeing its not a good place for me

to live, and improve, I would be a cruel Barbarian
of a Father, to leave my children behind,

I have never to my knowledge had any quarrel
with the Community principles nor doubted any of
its cardinal points till lately, which is the social
question, which of late has brought on to me
trouble respecting my children especially the two
Girls Grace & Ellen.

The principle cause that has brought a *doubt and
shade over my mind* is the looking towards the
centrel portion of the Community for *advice and
example* from that quarter my Faith has been
Shaken. There has been no woman in the Family
that has given me so hard a wound as you did while
with us or during your stay at Oneida, There has
been no woman in the Community that I have loved
so well as you, except one. There has been no
woman in the Family that I looked up to for Coun-
cil and example more than yourself.

I do not think I am to be blamed because I love a
woman. If the Lorde give me love, or a mesage or
a dispach, to cary to a woman I am only an agent,
or a dispach bearer, doing business for the Lorde,
And when a woman has been made acquainted with
the contents of the dispacth, or message, if she cant
respond to it, she is not to be blamed, But she can
be respectful, and womanly to the *dispacth, also to
the bearer.*

now then the disrespect, or ill treatment mani-
fested towards the *bearer*, is but a little consequence

compared to the message he bares is. Cruel and
disrespectful treatment shown to a message of love
that God has sent to an individual is one of the
greatest crimes known to man, The killing of the
Body is nothing in comparison The killing of the
affections is spiritual treason, and will meet with the
judgments of God.

I do not know that you have been very disrespectful to me in love matters but you have justified it in
others, especially in *philena* Philena has treated
me, (understand me now, *the mesage*,) with the most
cruelty and disrespect that I thought was posible
for a woman to do. And I feel justified in saying
she can assign no cause for it, out side of herself, I
have done every thing for that woman that was
posible for me to do in acts of kindness. I will refer
to a few, out of thousands, I would wash for her
when she was unable, a half day and would wash
up the dining room most always when she worked
there, and sometimes would right after, call in her
Room to spend a few minuts, but she would alway
turn me out of the room. I have Spent all day and
gone without my dinner and supper till after dark
in longe days many a time making a chest and some
things for her that she wanted, and in fetching them
to her and stopping fifteen minuts or so afterwards
she would leave the Room or give me to understand
she did not want me to stay, when it seems to me I
would have given a Hundred dollars to have stopped
with her a litle while, but no suffering or appeal that

I could make to her could move her more than you could move a stone, I have frequently told her I felt she was the only woman that I felt free to tell how I felt als said to her I felt I was improveing and growing strong in the Lord, & Community principles, while in good relations with her, but as soon as I turned way from her I felt condemned, and would recede from the Community, but she seemed to care nothing about it but took every insincere way she could to drive me from her and in a way I thought inposible for a civilised woman to do, especially one professing to be a witness of the establishment of the Kingdom of God, I have only named a few of her cruel acts towards me,

And I criticised this spirit in that letter that you condemn me for, and said in the letter the future would deside the just criticism of the letter, I said in that letter I felt it was rong for her always to take the un spiritual for her association such as Homer, but was willing to leave the future to deside it merit, And I was confident I had inspiration to give that criticism, and never have doubted from that time to this, But felt God would prove to me if I would wait in patience, now then my impression about philena and homer respecting there association, has proved true, The judment has come and its no use to deny it. when a person is brought to judgment for ther conduct its *disrespecful to God to hide the person from it by justification* * * * *
[Here follows a specification of the judgment which

Mills claim the credit of having brought on Philena
and Homer, which from motives of delicacy we
omit.] Also her lame foot [a sprained ankle] not
able to put it to the Floor—now then I have some
experience about her lameness For nearly three
years I have tried to dance with that woman, she
would from time to time promis to dance with me
and then go and dance with others I am most
asshamed to tell how much I have suffered or been
temped in this respect by her but I being a weak,
Br she aught not to made her weak Br stumble Its
my impression and I cannot get red of it, God is
displeased in the way she has saught her own pleasure in danseing, and cut her off from it—

Now then Mrs. Miller you may think I am con-
demning all the women but I dont feel to condemn
none, nor philena, nor you I believe you have, nor
phlena, have done all you could consistent with the
circumstances and condition of things, from the fact
it does not seem to me posible in the nature of
things that human beings professing to love God,
and each other could look on with impunity, and
know that they were killing the poor affections by
leaving them in prison, hungry naked thursty without being mooved with compassion, I say I am
tempted to beleeve the difficulty must ly in the
principle and not in the persons—

now Sister Miller I do pray God will bring me out
of this mire if possible, that I can be one with the
rest of you, and I pray also, that God will de-

mand my life immediately if I disturb a truthful principle that he has planted here to hold us together, I wis I could see you I beleeve it would do me me good I perhaps think more of you now then any other I feel Isolated from every one If you feel to answer the you may, sincerely yours

MR, MILLS

Sunday, Oct. 23, 1864.

Mrs H Skinner,

Dear Sister, its been a longe time I have *been very hard* and distance from you, and would not be reconciled to you, I have of late felt, if it were posible, I would break through such feellings, and try to feel towards you as I once did, I find in holding you off, and shuning you, I get no better feellings, I find I am effected with the same feelings to wards all your Family, I have ardently prayed the Lorde to remove such feellings from me, These thoughts has ocopied my attention, to ask you to come and stay with me one knight, not for secual purposes, but for spiritual interchange, If a friendly visit of this character, find acceptance in your feellings, I shall be happy to meet you—when fully considerd, please send me a note or otherwise inform me, Sincerily yours WM MILLS

MR. MILLS :—You must excuse me, for I think that would be no way to promote our fellowship. The way would be by your becoming a good man,

which I know you can be if you will. I have no
hard feelings toward you, but should rejoice if you
should prove to be a true brother.   II. II. S.

Let these samples of "communing" suffice for
the "marriage feast to which every dish is free to
every guest," at which Mills had been invited, and
then let us hear what Brother Noyes thinks about
the practical workings of his grand theory. It is
copied from the same issue of the paper:

"But a full view of his operations as a lover cannot
be obtained, without adverting to his special dealings
with young *girls*. For, strange and incredible as it
may seem to those who have heard his complaints
about the treatment of his daughters, and have wit-
nessed his "holy horror" at the dealings of the
Community with the young, he himself has had
more personal familiarity with the class of girls in
the Community that are just now passing the period
of puberty, than any other man. It is mortifying
to be obliged to confess a fact so discreditable to the
paternal care of the Community; but truth must
come out, and we offer as some excuse for our toleration of this vile intimacy, the fact, that for want of
systematic surveillance, the leading members of the
Community were, till very recently, entirely ignorant
of its existence.

*   *   *   *   *   *   *   *

"It might be expected that such a man would
keep a sharp eye on the girls in the Community,

and would seize any opportunity to make his way among them; especially after being generally rejected by the women. Opportunity was not wanting. In the first place, by right of invention he presided over his wonderful machinery for dish-washing, and so was a high functionary in the kitchen. This brought him into familiar contact with all the girls in the Community from those of twenty years old and downwards, dish-washing being one of the services assigned to them in a system of rotation. From such inquiries as our modesty has allowed us to make, we judge that he 'popped the question' or in some way made love to nearly every girl that served with him during his presidency of two or three years. And in the next place his youngest daughter, Grace, belonged to the class that are just now becoming young women (say from the age of sixteen and downwards), and was a leader among them. He assumed control of her and required her to frequent his room. The situation of his room in a rather secluded wing of an unimportant building, favored privacy. Grace, for reasons which will appear hereafter, was glad to bring with her to his room the whole of her class of girls. The result of these arrangements was that for several months in the Summer of 1863 (precisely how long we do not know) Mills had daily meetings with ten or twelve girls, of ages varying from 11 to 14, *with locked doors.* All this, as we have said, was unknown to the family generally at the time, and has

come to light by the free disclosures of these girls.
Mrs. Skinner thus reports a meeting for inquiry held
with them Dec. 30, 1864 :

" 'Ten of the girls met in my room this morning,
and told, one by one, of Mr. Mills' doings with
them, and the following is a true account :

" 'Summer before last, or about a year and a half
ago, they were in the frequent practice of going to
his room evenings and at other times. They first
began to go there because Grace wanted they should
go with her, and continued to go because it was a
place where they could 'carry on' and meet each
other without being criticised for being too much
alone together. They despised Mr. Mills, and at the
same time there was a fascination about his room.
He kept apples and pears and 'goodies' of various
kinds in his trunk for them, and often gave them
candies and sugar-plums. He kept *wine*, also, of
his own making, which he offered them, urging
them to drink. Isabella loved wine, and used to
drink it, but the other girls generally refused his in-
vitations ; Arabella used to tell him his wine did not
seem clean. He gave them also cologne and beads.
They all say that Grace seemed afraid to be with her
father alone—would never go to his room without
some of them with her, and was sure to leave when
they did, refusing to go back when he called her.
They have an impression that she was afraid of his
taking liberties with her. They say she *hated*
her father. Whenever two or three were there he

would always *lock the door*. Many times he has *pushed them on to the bed*, and they would have to scramble *over him* to get off. He would tease them to kiss him, and promise them candy if they would. He asked them to kiss him at other times and in other places besides his room; several of the girls said he had teased them to kiss him '*lots of times*.' One game that they had in his room was a kind of mock 'confession of Christ.' He would ask them to *confess Christ*; they would do it and laugh, and he would try to make them do it over soberly; then one would say, 'I will this time,' and then they would have another laugh. Another game was mock criticism. He would ask them to criticise him, and so go round calling on each one. They would tell him he was sickish, and walked with his head on one side, picked his teeth with his knife, &c.

"'Another way he had of amusing them was to tell over all the women that he loved, and tease them to tell what men they loved, guessing this man and that, so as to make them tell. He would say to them that he hadn't any secrets, and they ought to tell him, if he did them. He was fond of flattering them, telling them what pretty girls they were—remarking about their looks. His talk with them was mostly about *private* matters.

"'Consuelo and Isabella and Arabella were the most free with him. Consuelo started a practice they had of carrying him presents. They would get

up a basket full of trifles and have a great deal of
sport seeing him look them over. One time he was
writing to Charles Mills and asked them to write to
him ; so they would write one line and he one.

" 'He asked Arabella to stay with him twice. This
was done within the last year. He talked with her
a good deal the last Summer—always about sexual
matters—love affairs in the Community. For instance, he would say that he could not get near
Helen N., because Mr. B. kept so close to her. He
would speak of Mrs. R.'s baby, what a pretty little
thing she was, and then say "if he could get the
woman he loved he would have a baby, and that his
time was coming yet." Mr. Mills was in the habit
of telling the girls how neat he was, that he changed
his shirt six times a week, that his bed was clean,
&c.

" 'The girls say they were in the way of similar
freedom with William Mills, the son—going into his
room—sitting in his lap, and having high times.' "

" Most of these girls were in untouched maiden-
hood. The three named as most familiar with Mills,
were sexually unknown to the men of the Community. The girl to whom Mills talked most about
having babies, and whom he urged again and again
to come to his bed was only thirteen years old,
scarcely a woman, certainly a virgin—a blooming
combination of fun and bashfulness.

"This Satanic school, secret as it was, produced
effects on the character of the girls which were very

visible and notorious in the family. It is safe to say
that the Community has had more trouble from the
perversity, insubordination, and frivolous habits of
this one generation of young ladies than from all the
rest of the children that it has brought up. For a
long time they grew more and more willful and dis-
sipated, they became a burden, almost of despair,
to their mothers and teachers. Some mysterious
perverting enchantment seemed to be upon them
which alienated them from the Community and from
all righteousness, till they became a serious nuisance
to the whole family. They were most of them born
in the Community, or at least had been brought up
there from early childhood."

*   *   *   *   *   *   *   *   *

"Such facts as these will help honest outsiders
to conceive of the difficulties and perplexities which
the leading members of the Community have been
under in respect to the social education of the young,
and especially the girls. Our greatest reason for
regret has been that we have not had wisdom and
power of attraction enough to save them from such
spells and snares of the devil.   J. H. N."

With the works before us we might go on at any
length with just such a string of beastliness until
the reader would cloy. Our space forbids it, therefore we will cut it short where it is, with one or two
observations.

From the above it will be seen that it makes some

difference in that "Kingdom on Earth" in the person who seeks to partake of his "dish" so liberally provided. The green-eyed monster is as much at work to-day in Oneida Community as he was ten years since, but no internecine strife has been sufficiently violent to throw it to the surface, except in one or two important instances. The whole tenor of their tirade against Mills, as can be ascertained by those who wish to trouble themselves with research, impinges on the amount he was to have in settlement, and not on any moral ground, as they are all equally guilty with him of the crimes charged.

The intelligent reader will consider what we have already furnished a sufficient exposé of the moral character of those who go to make up Oneida Community, and nothing more was intended. We will therefore close this chapter with the funny side of this controversy. Here is a specimen letter of condolence from a former member :

"About the time Mills was 'put out,' I received a letter from Oneida, saying, 'he came down stairs, one bearing an arm, another a leg, crying murder at the top of his voice.' I was just wicked enough to add in my answer, that the people all stood by, closed their ears, and smiled, saying one to another this must be what military men call a flank ' moove'-ment. Poor man, he has suffered everything but death (pity he couldn't that) for the last five years. Who can tell the *troubles and trials he did have to enjoy*, and all for those hard-hearted women ? Just imagine his feelings, loving them e'en just to death, but obliged to stand by at a cotillion and see Homer get all the sly kisses. Who wonders that the 'old man' was stirred up within, and that he should cry out with the poet Rip Van Winkle,

'Lodl lodlclmi komo kum,
Lanki spanki locofoco bum !'

Which means—

I would not live alway, I ask not to stay,
Where women don't like me and push me away.

Or in other words—

I would not live always, I'll be darned if I can,
Rejected by women, and hated by man."

CHAPTER VII.

Burial of their Dead—An Applicant Rejected—Numbers Increasing—A Fitting Finale.

The members of Oneida Community do not die ;
according to their idea of death, when one of their
number "shuffles off the mortal coil," he has only
been summoned from the "Kingdom of Heaven" on
earth, established by the sainted Noyes and the
Cragin family, to that other land "from whose
bourne no traveler ever returns." They say that—
"The pall of the fear of death which overspreads
all the world, is removed from our abode. We are
all conscious of the fact, by whatever means it has
come about, and it is having a tremendous influence
upon our character. Strength, ambition, hope, have
ten times the chance to flourish. Healthy merriment
is not checked by the ghostly spectre. Our happiness never feels its chill. Age does not rest on its
oars and wait for it, but wends back as fast as possible to immortal youth. ' To be prepared for death,'
never enters our heads ; and a visitor from some
sphere where it is not known, might go in and out
with us ever so long, and not have his curiosity excited about this point in human destiny."

And so there is no such thing as a funeral known
to them. A suitable coffin is provided for the re-

mains, not a prayer is raised nor a dirge chanted, and only enough attend the interment to perform the actual labor incident to the occasion. That their belief in this respect may be more fully understood, we quote from the Perfectionist, Vol. IV., No. 13, where Noyes says :

"As it has been frequently reported that I have professed a belief that I should 'never die,' I may as well briefly define here my position in relation to this point. The conclusions to which I came, at the period under consideration, and which I have always avowed since, are as follows :

"1. As Christ did not scruple to say, ' He that believeth on me shall never die,' and that too with manifest reference of some kind to the body (see John 11:26 and 8:51), so the believer need not scruple to apply that language to himself. If then I am pressed to say whether I take the language literally or figuratively, I answer, Neither way, but *spiritually*. The believer may part with his flesh and blood, but shall never part with his life. His true body—that which is within his flesh and blood—is already risen from the dead by the power of Christ's resurrection, and parting with flesh and blood will be to him no death. He will pass into the inner mansions, not naked but clothed with his immortal body.

"2. The death of flesh and blood to the believer is not *inevitable*. It is not a 'debt' which he owes to the devil, or to sin, or to the laws of nature.

His debts to all these tyrants are paid. Christ has bought him out of their hands; and the question whether he shall die in the ordinary sense will be determined, not by some inexorable necessity, but by the choice of Christ, and of course by the choice of himself as a member of Christ. 'No man taketh my life from me (said Christ), but I lay it down of myself."—(John 10:18.) The power which he had in respect to his own life, he has in respect to the lives of those who believe on him. As members of him, they may lay down their lives as he did; but no man or devil takes their lives from them. Accordingly Paul, balancing between the desire of life and death, said, '*I wot not which I shall* choose'—(Phil. 1:22.) This language implies that life and death were at his option. The fact that the saints who lived till the Second Coming (to say nothing of Enoch and Elijah) passed within the vale without dying, proves that the death of flesh and blood is not inevitable—that Christ has power to discharge believers from its bond.

"3. It is certain from the predictions of scripture that the time is coming when death will be abolished both as to form and substance in this world. It is not to be expected that indivduals will enter into this last victory of Christ much in advance of the whole body of believers. God is evidently preparing for a *general* insurrection against the 'king of terrors,' and we may reasonably anticipate the crisis and victory as near. 'They that are alive and remain' till the promised consummation, will not die in any sense, but will pass from the mortal to the immortal state by a change similar to that which is described in I. Cor., 15:51, &c.

" My profession, then, since 1834, has been briefly this : ' If I pass through the form of dying, yet in fact I shall never die. Yet I am not a debtor to the devil even in regard to the form of dying. No man taketh my life from me. I wot not whether I shall choose life or death. But this I know, that if I live till the kingdom of God comes, which I believe is near, I shall never die in fact or in form. This is the profession, for which I have been charged by certain 'devout and honorable women' with 'stumping my Maker.'

" The first results of the act of faith which I have described, were delightful. I passed one night in unspeakable happiness. I felt that I had burst through the shroud of death into the 'heavenly places.' "

The novelty of the following letter has induced us to throw it in incidentally :

Boston, Mass., Mar. 20, 1875.

SIRS :—You will remember me as J. Shedd—who made application to become a member of the Oneida Community ; but I thank God from the bottom of my heart for being refused. Since I came home my eyes have been opened to the danger I was in. Had you accepted me, you would have secured one more soul for hell. I will thank God every day of my life for having delivered me from the company of such hogs. I did not give my right name, nor will I give it now.   J. SHEDD.

That is the way! When Mr. Shedd was here he so persistently begged to join, that we could with difficulty get rid of him. He was in a monstrous hurry. We said No! His letter shows that we did wisely. Evidently something beside religion sent him here.—*Ed. Circular.*

So shrewdly and cunningly have the Communists reared their institution that they now openly boast of its impregnability against the outside world. In speaking of the death-rate in their midst from nervous diseases, this fact is strongly hinted at. They say in the *Circular* of Nov. 7, 1870, that, "As the Oneida Communists have now won almost universal recognition as lovers of industry, good order and intelligence, it is reasonable to conclude that their successors will escape some portion of the trials which they have endured, and consequently that the proportion of members afflicted with nervous diseases will become less as the years pass on."

Notwithstanding the assertion of their organ, that "the parent Community at Oneida is full," and "it wants no more," their number has increased, during less than six months, from 205 to 253; and this increase could not possibly come from births among them, as the number of adult females among them capable of child-bearing precludes such a possibility. It comes, then, from the outside world, and its significance is of the gravest importance. While their journal is throwing sand in the eyes of the world, the members are secretly proselyting and augmenting both their numbers and their wealth—fortifying their stronghold against the time when the laws which they are daily transgressing shall call them to account.

We copy the following article concerning this institution (from the trenchant pen of Prof. Mears, of Hamilton College, Clinton, N. Y.) as a fitting conclusion. It was copied from the *Watchword*, a paper published at Ilion, N. Y.:

The fabled upas had its own poison as its best defense. The disagreeable creature that prowls around our barnyard at night is comparatively secure from attack by its very offensiveness. There are doctrines and practices in society which owe their safety to their very noisomeness. No circle of decent people could sit still and listen to the description of the Oneida Community as drawn from their own public documents These columns are not and cannot be opened to the vileness deliberately planned and perpetrated and defended by these self-styled Perfectionists. Hence the difficulty of any popular exposure of the nuisance.

Yet who had any love for the upas tree, because its exhalations forbade his near approach and scrutiny? Who needed to go very near it to convince

himself of its deadly nature? And who that learns
only in the most general way the facts in regard to
the flagrant immoralities of Oneida Community, does
not share in the indignation at its continued existence? A close acquaintance ought not surely to be
needed to set our entire religious and moral population energetically to work, abating the nuisance and
uprooting it from our soil. Do we need to know
anything more of the Oneida Community than that
the laws of marriage are systematically set at naught
there, and that men and women, young and old, are
banded together for the purpose of establishing an
order of things subversive of the family, and turning
the relation of the sexes into a ministry of lust and
degradation? Surely, it is not necessary to take the
roof off of their great abode, and parade all their
abominable doings before the public eye, in order to
reach and rouse the moral sentiment of the people.
[And yet the exterior is so fair, there is such order,
neatness and thrift about the establishment, so much
has been said of the business capacity and of the
products of the industry of the Community, its
good side has been made so prominent, that there is
reason to believe that a presentation of the ugly
side of the affair has become necessary. For twenty-
seven years, the people of the centre of New York
have been suffering themselves to become accus-
tomed to this moral monstrosity. It has grown familiar. Its evil aspects and peculiarities have
ceased to strike them. A large part of the popula-

tion neighboring the Community have become interested in its business operations, and selfishly wishes it prosperity, and is ready to protest against any interference with its regular working for any reason whatever. It is almost ludicrous to see how a few thousand dollars' worth of canned fruit, some thousands of racoon and bear traps, and a few hundred weight of twisted silk, representing the work of a factory employing about two hundred hands, can warp public opinion in regard to a matter of the deepest moral significance. Almost any little mountain stream in our well-watered Central New York can boast of half a dozen organized industries as important to the general interest of trade as the Oneida Community. And yet there are editors of journals considered respectable, who can become almost pathetic over the possible injury that might arise to the petty interests by agitating the question of interfering with immoralities of the Community.

*　　*　　*　　*　　*　　*　　*　　*　　*

Here, in the heart of the Empire State, in sight of some of its most famous schools, colleges and churches, amid its most cultivated population, is an institution avowedly at war with the foundation principles of our domestic and civil order, a set of men banded together for the purpose of practicing shameful immoralities, and leading the young of both sexes who unfortunately happen to come under their care into similar impure and shocking practices, and teaching them that moral and religious perfection justify and command them. Here are men and women who announce as part of their creed *the sinfulness of the marriage relation ;* who recommend a more unrestricted association of the sexes; who invent impure devices by which the lustful desires may be gratified without any inconvenient results; who put the sexual instincts of men upon a level with those of brutes, by their plan of raising a breed of men as a breed of cattle is raised ; who prevent the formation of those powerful and tender attachments which give the relationship of home, husband, wife, mother, child, brother and sister their intense significance, and make them talismans of energy and activity; the automic forces, mighty and subtle, which binds the whole fabric of society together, and constitutes the fair remnants of Paradise which are left to fallen man upon earth.

These are not overdrawn strokes of rhetoric; their bold and loathsome truth may be found in the printed documents which the Community are publishing and circulating every day among those who will take the trouble to ask or pay for them. The good people of Central New York have no business to tolerate this vileness at their very doors. The people of Putney, Vermont, where the Community originated, could not abide them, and drove them out twenty-seven years ago. If Central New York is inferior to Vermont in sound morality, its silence and toleration are perfectly inscrutable. The people

of Illinois could not endure the immorality of the
Mormons, but drove them from Nauvoo in 1846, and
compelled them to take refuge in the great central
basin, a thousand miles from the outskirts of civilization. Thus polygamy was treated, while the far
more corrupt concubinage of Oneida Community
luxuriates in ease in the heart of New York State,
enjoys the compliments of one portion of the newspaper press, and the silent acquiescence of another
portion, uses the United States mails for the circula-
tion of its poisonous literature, is visited by throngs
of the curious or the indifferent, by pic-nic parties
organized for the purpose, and even by Sunday-
school excursions.

This is the way we treat such offenders in N. Y.
State, and our leniency is understood and apprecia-
ted by this kind of people. Within a few days we
have learned that another party of free lovers are
preparing to take advantage of it; a party whose
principles are far looser than those of Oneida Community. The Oneida Community have prepared an
ingenious little outline map of the State of N. Y.,
with a circle drawn so that the circumference touches
the extreme southern, western and northern corners
of the State. The Community itself forms the center
of this circle. The new establishment is on the circumference; just where this imaginary line touches
the northern corner of the State, on Valcour Island,
opposite Plattsburg, on Lake Champlain, this new
and worse edition of the nuisance propose to settle.

According to the Plattsburg *Sentinel*, quoted in the Utica *Herald* of Sept. 28, eight hundred acres of land have been purchased on the island, besides a fruit farm on the opposite shore of Vermont ; even the price of the latter, $26,000, is specified.

The great fundamental feature of the organization, it is said, is free love in its most unrestricted form.

The name of the chief mover in this enterprise is given as Colonel John Wilcox, of Omro, Wis., and it is stated that the advance guard, twelve in number, left Chicago for the island on the 20th of August. The Plattsburg paper disposes of the moral aspects of the affair in the following flippant way:

"We do not expect that the establishment of this colony within a few miles of Plattsburg will be considered as a special honor, although we presume if it prospers like the Oneida Community it will be quite an additional attraction to excursionists, and give Valcour Island a wide-spread reputation."

If any proof were needed of the general demoralizing effect of the continued toleration of such establishments upon the tone of public sentiment in the State, this newspaper extract would furnish it. In place of indignant remonstrance we have a careless, good-humored acceptance of the fact as settled. A passing allusion to the possible discredit of the affair to the neighborhood is balanced by reckoning the advantages likely to follow from its establishment.

Shortly after the publication of Prof. Mears' article, the Valcour Island establishment collapsed for want of funds, and its deluded victims returned to their homes. We now ask, how long will Oneida Community endure? Truly,

> " Vice is a monster of such hideous mien,
> That, to be hated, needs but to be seen.
> But seen too oft—familiar with its face,
> We first endure—then pity—then embrace."

THE END.

www.ingramcontent.com/pod-product-compliance
Lightning Source LLC
Chambersburg PA
CBHW020808020726
47495CB00008B/2635